I0746538
Spartan + FRIENDS

Hazel and Spartan's Beach Adventure
Colouring and Literacy Book

Consolidating phonics knowledge with extended decodable text.

Word Count
Approx. 462 words

ch → children, cheerful, beach
sh → splash, shore, brushed, shone, shout
or → snort
aw → saw, draw, pawed
th → with, the, then, their

High-Frequency Words
as, his, her, up, get, went, then, when, their, them, be, had
they, he, she, we, was, said, all, your, you, I, that, this, out

Irregular Words
said, your, you, are, was, they, their, come, some, one, done, two

Practice Words
Spartan, Suki, Huxley, float, tack, reins, helmet, stride, trot / trotted
dolphin, seaside, snorted, pricked, splash / splashed, spray, stomped
giggle / giggled, foamy, glow, tide

Teacher Prep Before Reading
Review diagraphsay (play, spray, away)
ea (beach, sea, neat)

Practice igh triagraph: (bright, delight)

Vocabulary support: Introduce float (horse trailer), tack, reins,
seaside, tide, stride, dolphin, splash, spray, foam.

Hazel woke up with a grin so bright,
"We're riding the horses at the beach today, right?"
Spartan was ready and keen to go,
his hooves went clip-clop as she led him slow.

Huxley came running, pulling his boots on tight,
Suki, spotty and lively, was prancing with delight.
Their parents had packed the gear with care,
float hitched to the car, time to go
they would soon be there.

Huxley led Suki clip-clop down the track,
the horses were loaded, doors closed at the back.
"It's time to go to the beach at last,
with blue-green waves rolling wide and fast."

The beach was wide, the tide slipped low,
the sun on the water gave a golden glow.
Mum parked the car, she smiled with pride,
"Time to tack up for your seaside ride!"

Hazel brushed Spartan, sleek and tall,
his mane like silk, the finest of all.
Huxley tied Suki and picked out her feet,
then placed the saddle, secure and neat.

Reins in hand, helmets on heads,
"Up you get," Mum cheerfully said.
Spartan snorted, proud and bold,
Suki pawed at the sand of gold.

They started off with a gentle stride,
the horses steady, side by side.
Soon they trotted, the pace grew fast,
laughing together as waves rolled past.

The tide rolled in with a whoosh and roar,
salt on their lips, hooves on the shore.
Hazel edged closer, her laughter clear,
Huxley joined in with a happy cheer.

Spartan stepped into the water blue,
he stomped and splashed, the spray he threw!
Suki danced and joined the play,
the waves leapt high in a foamy spray.

The children giggled, their faces bright,
the horses shone in the morning light.
"Look at Spartan!" Hazel cried,
"He loves the sea and the rising tide!"

Huxley grinned as Suki played,
"she wants to splash in the waves he made!"
The horses stomped, the water flew,
it sparkled white, green and blue.

When play was done, they turned once more,
riding back along the shore.
Their parents waved from far away,
pleased to see their children play.

Hazel looked out to the deep sea,
something moved as quick as can be.
A dolphin leapt with a splash so high,
it twisted and turned in the bright blue sky.

The children stopped to watch it play,
it danced in the waves then swam away.
Spartan stood tall, his ears pricked high,
Suki snorted as the waves rolled by.

"Goodbye, dolphin!" the children sang,
their voices bright as the sea breeze rang.
The sun shone warm, the tide all the way in,
it was time for home, with happy grins.

Back at the float, gear packed with care,
the children smiled at the fun they'd share.
"Beach rides are magic," Hazel cried,
"Next time let's bring all our friends to ride!"

Activities (for after reading)

1. Re-read the story and circle words with ay (play, spray, away)

2. Find and <u>underline</u> all the words with ar (Spartan)

3. Write 3 new sentences with words that start with s (splash)

____

____

____

____

____

____

____

4. Can you copy the sound of Spartan's hooves: clip-clop?

5. Fill the gap: "A _______________ leapt with a splash so high."

Activities (for after reading)

6.Write a new ending about what else Hazel and Huxley might have seen or done at the beach.

____

____

____

____

____

____

____

____

____

____

Activities (for after reading)

7. Write some words that rhyme with, glow:

____

____

8. Can you name three things that you might find at the beach?

____

____

____

9. What was the most fun part for the children do you think, playing in the waves or watching the dolphin? Why?

____

____

____

____

Activities (for after reading)

10. Can you retell the important parts of the story?

____

____

11. What was your favourite part of story?

____

____

____

12. Imagine the beach, what else might you see there?
Draw a picute of what you image below:

Activities (for after reading)

13. Draw a line back to the phonics sound that matches the word

ar sound   **sh sound**

brush   *car*

far   *Spartan*

splash   *fish*

14. Complete the words with the missing sounds:

fl ___ t
r ___ ns
sh___e
b___ch
s___side
h____ves

15. Colour in all of the story pages.

Spartan + FRIENDS